Mr and Mrs Hay the Horse

by ALLAN AHLBERG

with pictures by
COLIN McNAUGHTON

Puffin

Viking

PUFFIN/VIKING

Published by the Penguin Group
Penguin Books Ltd, 27 Wrights Lane, London W8 5TZ, England
Penguin Books USA Inc., 375 Hudson Street, New York, New York 10014, USA
Penguin Books Australia Ltd, Ringwood, Victoria, Australia
Penguin Books Canada Ltd, 10 Alcorn Avenue, Toronto, Ontario, Canada M4V 3B2
Penguin Books (NZ) Ltd, Cnr Rosedale and Airborne Roads, Albany, Auckland, New Zealand

Penguin Books Ltd, Registered Offices: Harmondsworth, Middlesex, England

Published by Viking 1981
5 7 9 10 8 6

Published in Puffin Books 1981
15 17 19 20 18 16

Text copyright © Allan Ahlberg, 1981
Illustrations copyright © Colin McNaughton, 1981

Educational Advisory Editor: Brian Thompson

Printed in Singapore by Imago Publishing
Set in Century Schoolbook by Filmtype Services Limited, Scarborough

ISBN Paperback 0 14 03.1247 1
ISBN Hardback 0–670–80573–4

Mr and Mrs Hay were a horse.
Mr Hay was the front end.
Mrs Hay was the back end.
They worked in a circus,
and on the stage.

Now Mr and Mrs Hay
had not always been a horse.
When they first met,
Mr Hay was a tree
and Mrs Hay was a chicken.

But soon they fell in love,
got married –
and bought a horse-suit.

As the years went by,
Mr and Mrs Hay had two children.
There was a boy named Henry.
There was a girl named Henrietta.
When the children were little,
they were very happy.

They rode on their mum and dad's back.
They laughed
at their mum and dad's tricks.
They were as proud as could be.
"Our mum and dad are a horse!"
they told everybody.

But later on,
when the children were older –
the trouble began.

Henry and Henrietta were embarrassed
by their mum and dad.
The trouble was, Mr and Mrs Hay
liked being a horse.
They went everywhere
in their horse-suit.
They liked doing tricks too.
They liked galloping about.

Other mums and dads
were more sensible.
The mums wore dresses
and cooked apple pies.
The dads dug the gardens
and took the dogs for a walk.

Mr and Mrs Hay did not
take their dog for a walk.
They took him for a ride!

So Henry and Henrietta
tried to get their parents
to be like other parents.
"Would you like a job in an office, Dad?"
they said.

"Would you like to work
in a shop, Mum?"
They also hid the horse-suit.
But it was no use.
The horse-suit was soon found.
And things did not get better,
they got worse.

There was trouble at school too.
Other mums and dads
came to see the teacher,
and waited quietly.

Mr and Mrs Hay
came to see the teacher –
and galloped about.

Now once a year at the school
there was a Christmas Show.
A conjuror came and
did his tricks for the children.
The mums and dads were also invited.

Henry and Henrietta were pleased
about the show.
But they were worried too.
"Oh dear," they said.
"The other mums and dads
will come in their best clothes
and be sensible.
Our mum and dad will be galloping
round in a horse-suit!"

They helped to get the stage ready.
They put the chairs out.

On the night of the show
Henry and Henrietta went to
school early.

By half-past seven most of the people
were in their seats.

But Mr and Mrs Hay were late.
Henry and Henrietta
could not see them anywhere.

Then the headmaster stepped
onto the stage.
He was looking worried.
"Ladies and gentlemen, boys and girls!"
he said.

"I am sorry to say
there will be no show tonight!"
A baby in the front row
began to cry.
"The conjuror cannot come,"
the headmaster said.
"He had to take his rabbits to the vet."

Now all the mums and dads looked sad.
The children looked sad too.
The baby in the front row
cried louder than ever.
Then, suddenly, there was
the sound of a galloping horse and
onto the stage came Mr and Mrs Hay!

"Oh dear," said Henry and Henrietta.
They felt their cheeks
getting hot and red.
But soon Mr and Mrs Hay
were doing their tricks.
They sang songs too;

and danced – and told jokes!
Then the baby in the front row
began to laugh.
And the children laughed.
And the parents cheered
and clapped their hands.

Henry and Henrietta
began to feel better.
When the headmaster said,
"Three cheers for Mr and Mrs Hay!"
they felt better still.

Bravo!

Hooray!

More!

When the other children said,
"We wish *our* mums and dads
were horses!"
Henry and Henrietta were as proud
as could be!

And now this story is nearly ended
– except for one more thing.
Two nights later,
when Henry and Henrietta
were fast asleep,
a funny Father Christmas
crept into their room.
This Father Christmas had
lots of presents for the children –
lots and lots.
But there was one special present.
It was just what Henry and Henrietta
wanted most of all...

...a little horse-suit!

The End